Terry the Tree
and the
Accidental Giant

ELENA VENTURA

Gerry the tree loves the environment he lives in. Surrounded by lush greenery and blue skies, people are nice and friendly, and so are the animals that come and visit most days.

Birds build their nest on his branches and he would look after the baby birds while the parents look for food.

His favourite friends, Dorothy and Boo would come and play under his shade, and sometimes their little friends would join them too.

Terry, however, hopes to become taller, as he looks up admiring the taller trees around him.
Maybe someday he would become taller too, and he would be able to see farther beyond.

Then one day, it happened.

He found himself becoming bigger and taller, and soon he was looking down from the treetops, and the houses are looking smaller from the distance down below.

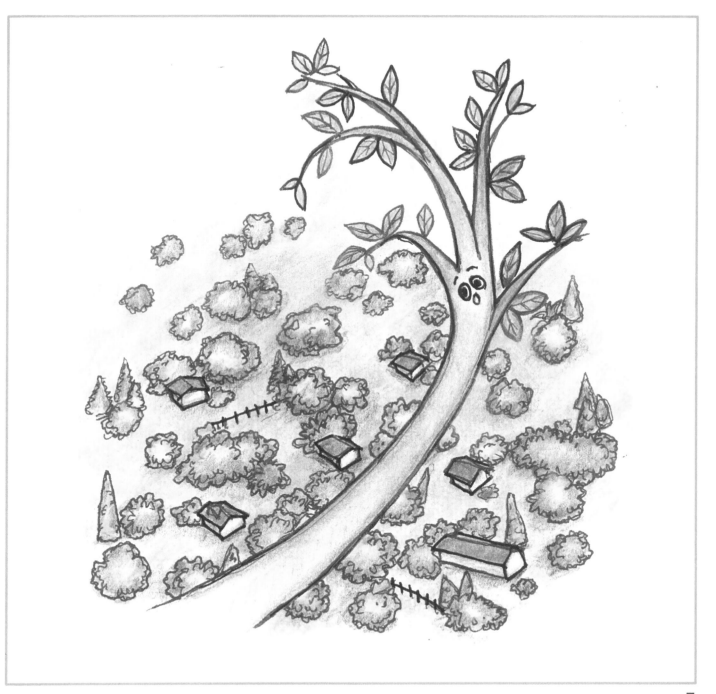

Soon he could not see anything else but fluffy clouds around him and the huge open space above. He started feeling dizzy.

Then something appeared from a distance among the clouds that looked like a huge pair of eyes staring at him.

And then a big voice - "Who's there? Is there anyone there?"

PAMELA'S GARDEN

Deep in the forest lives
a forest fairy named
Pamela in a wonderful
garden that no one else
has ever been except
for some forest
animals that the
fairy cares for.
Different plants
and flowers
abound
in stunning
colours and
everything
feels peaceful
and idyllic.

One part of the garden features an array of beautiful bonsai plants mounted on rocks that are used as plinths for the collection.

Pamela treasures her bonsai plants more than anything else in her garden.

THE LOST BUSHWALKER

A bushwalker, named Hugh, have been walking for days, getting deeper into the woods and have become aware that he was lost, but was determined to go on to find his way.

He had been surviving on fruit and berries and whatever else he could find, so when he spotted a rabbit he thought he might have a stew for a change.

He tried to catch the rabbit, unaware that a snake was watching him. When he got closer, the snake playfully snatched his hat, and Hugh instinctively tried to snatch it back, but a bird suddenly appeared and plucked the hat from the snake's grip and flew away with it. Forgetting about the rabbit, he gave chase to the bird which led him to a creek where the bird dropped the hat into the water.

Hugh then tried to retrieve his hat with a sigh.
Then, after having a drink from the creek
decided to have a rest.

He found a good spot under a tree and fell asleep. He must have slept for hours and into the night, and woke up blinded by a shaft of light coming through the canopy of trees from the morning sun.

Feeling better after a good rest, he felt ready to continue to go on his way, hoping to find more berries along the way.

After a long walk, he found a clearing up ahead where there was more sun and found himself in a place that didn't seem a part of the forest at all. The place displays a variety of stunning blooms and amazing plants he thought he may have walked right into a paradise.

He was unaware that he had intruded into Pamela's garden.

He wandered around and soon discovered the collection of miniature trees that he recognized as bonsai plants. Some are laden with fruit and some others with flowers. He was awed by the colourful blooms and the luscious looking fruit on such small trees.

He could not resist plucking some of the fruit and eating those.

All of a sudden he realized that he was bursting out of his clothes and becoming bigger uncontrollably. Looking around him, he was soon looking down from the treetops and everything else have become lower down below.

His now outgrown clothing are lying down on his feet on the ground.

He has now realized that he had become a giant.

Dazed and upset and trying to understand his situation, he absently wandered, not knowing what to do. He kept walking aimlessly among the trees, confused and trying to find some answers, until he found himself in a small community.
Surprised by the presence of the giant, the local people panicked and ran screaming for their lives.

Back in the woods, the forest fairy emerged and
found the discarded clothing on the ground.
She also found that some of the fruit on her prized
bonsai plants have been picked and eaten.

Pamela has now figured out that an intruder had been in her garden and stolen some of the fruit from her bonsai plant which may have possibly turned the intruder into a giant unknowingly. But when she found her pet turtle hurt on the ground, she became upset and determined to find and confront the culprit.

It didn't take long for Pamela to notice the commotion going on beyond and find the giant towering among the trees. She confronted the giant and showed him what had been done to her pet turtle.

Pamela became angrier when she saw that the turtle had now died, and decided to punish the giant.
She put a spell on the giant, casting him into the clouds where he had been condemned to stay until someone with a kind heart may find and save him.

Hugh suddenly found himself among the clouds and was distraught, feeling hopeless and desperate, not knowing what to do.

He has now become aware that there is nothing
he could do with his situation, and that he had
to live his fate until someone finds him.
He pondered helplessly if there is any possible
solution, but then who could possibly find him up
in the clouds, let alone save him.
He resigned himself to whatever is left of his
life to be nothing but misery and loneliness.
So he decided to sleep off his desperation,
hoping that this may only be a bad dream.

He didn't know how long he had been
sleeping when he was wakened by the sound
of rustling leaves.
But there is no one there.
No one.
Except for some branches from a tree that have
come up through the clouds.

Terry the tree can hardly believe that he had reached the clouds.
A huge pair of eyes was staring at him, and soon there was a face. Then a huge figure appeared, asking repeatedly in a big voice - "Is there anyone there? Has anyone come to save me?"

A heavy thud on the ground startled Terry. It was a bushwalker who laid down his backpack and sat heavily beside it, then leaned on Terry's trunk to rest.

The man sat there for a while and had a drink of water, then appeared to take a nap.

Having rested, the man stood up and studied
his surroundings, after which he looked up at the
tree, then gave it a gentle tap on the trunk as
though to thank him before turning to walk to
continue his journey.
Terry now had a good look at the bushwalker and
thought he looked familiar.
Indeed, he looked liked the giant he had seen
from the clouds.

His friends Dorothy and Boo soon came
running towards him to play.
Terry was so glad to be with his friends again.

END

Lightning Source UK Ltd.
Milton Keynes UK
UKHW050439020522
402290UK00002B/56